Lightning's Tale

The Story of a Wild Trout

Dedication
For my Dad—
who instilled in me a love of fly fishing and
for my wife, Lorli—
who has not only encouraged my fly fishing
and painting but paddled the canoe as well.

Acknowledgments

I would like to acknowledge the help received from John Claussen and Rich Kern of the Vermont Fish and Wildlife Department. Any errors in word or pictures are mine, however.

A special thanks to Lisa Beach, art teacher par excellence, who enabled and encouraged a brash beginner to pursue the dream of illustrating this book.

Many thanks go also to Trish Halloran, who tirelessly retyped the manuscript.

Of the many family members who provided helpful criticism, no one was more supportive and encouraging than my wife, Lorli. For them all, I am most grateful.

1994 • Hugh Campbell • Illustrations: Hugh Campbell
Book Design: Charlie Clifford

Printed in Hong Kong

Frank Amato Publications
P.O. Box 82112, Portland, Oregon 97282
(503) 653-8108 • FAX: (503) 653-2766
ISBN: 1-57188-199-9 UPC: 0-66066-00155-9
10 9 8 7 6 5 4 3 2

Kersploosh!

Kersploosh! A bucketful of wriggling, silver trout splashed into the stream and scattered, looking for their familiar pool. But here, it was all so different from the hatchery. Boulders, rocks and a rushing current replaced the shallow pool they had known all their lives.

Near a boulder and the bubbling current was a rainbow trout somewhat larger than the others. This was his home. He had the best place in that pool to catch food without swimming hard. In fact, he hardly swam at all, yet he stayed right next to the main current where the food floated by. An eddy was holding him next to a large rock. From time to time his fins and tail would move, and almost magically, he'd rise to the surface, eat something, and return to his post.

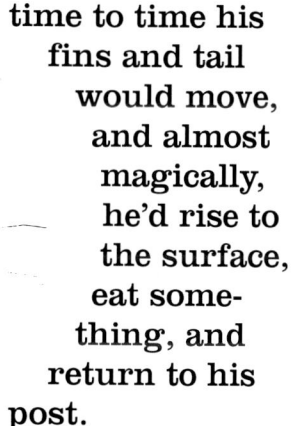

Handling that gusty current was no problem, either. He was at home in the mountain stream. He had grown up in it: he was a wild, native rainbow. He had learned how to avoid danger. Even his colors made him blend in with the rocks, the shadows and the running water.

The dark green on his back shaded into silver on his sides and belly. From his reddish gill covers a light pink streak ran down his side to his spotted, dark green tail. He wasn't easy to see in the stream. His shadow on the bottom was often the easiest way to find him.

He was a handsome young trout with dash and determination. When he went for food he usually got it. Not much escaped him.

The current carried the newcomers from the hatchery helter-skelter downstream between the rocks. The silvery fish swam hard to cross it to find calmer water where they could catch their breath.

Some went to the tail of the pool where the water flowed slower. There they could more easily inspect what was being carried along on the surface. They sampled some of the floating insects and those below the surface film that were unable to get away from them.

Other trout tried the head of the pool. There the current was stronger but with many more insects bubbling along. The trout tired quickly trying to catch them in the strong current.

By the time the sun had set, the hatchery trout realized that they hadn't caught much all day long. Now they were no longer scared: they were just hungry. But the familiar thump of a man's foot on the bank never came. No one showered down food pellets for them to gobble up. Now the young trout had to learn to find their own food in a foreign stream. They would soon learn about the currents and how to use them to their advantage. What they didn't know yet, was how to avoid being someone else's dinner.

Growing Up Wary

The native rainbow trout, who had never known the easy living of the hatchery, had grown up in the hurly-burly life of the stream. Ever since he could remember, he had been avoiding those who wanted to eat him.

He had started life as an egg in the gravel four springs ago. From the egg he had developed an inch long, sliver-like body with an egg sack still attached to his belly. This egg supplied him with all the food he needed for his first weeks. His main concern was to avoid the many mouths that were waiting for him to come out into the open. So he took shelter between the rocks and the rough gravel where he could swim and where those mouths couldn't reach him. By the time his egg sack had been used up he looked like a minnow or "fry" as they are called. He found lots to eat and learned to be a fast swimmer. By outswimming the others he could eat more and hide more quickly. He soon had earned the name, "Lightning".

By the banks of the stream he found many insects that tasted good. Nymphs bumbled around in the gravel. They didn't swim fast and didn't try hard to get away. They came in all shapes, colors and sizes. Some even came camouflaged as bundles of tiny twigs, but when he bit on them there was a juicy insect inside.

As the summer wore on there were times when there seemed to be a never-ending flow of insects coming down the current for him to eat. He was growing to be a respectable fry. Then there were times when he had one close call after another.

One day a kingfisher dove into the water beside him with a great ker-splash and carried off in his bill the fry that had been swimming right next to Lightning.

That commotion attracted the attention of a big, brown trout that suddenly appeared, mouth open. Lightning just made it into a narrow crevice between two rocks.

Later that same day he was swimming with other fry in the shallows when they noticed two green, root-like legs rising from the gravel to the surface and above. As the fry swam by, a long sharp bill darted down into the water, caught a trout around the middle and just as suddenly, flew up out of the water. That scared Lightning enough that he stayed hidden between a rock and boulder 'til nightfall.

Spring Rains

One day the sky grew gray, the surface of the water dimpled; it was raining. Whenever the surface became all wrinkled like that, Lightning felt more secure swimming in the open. He could only see a blurr above the water. His enemies couldn't see him below the surface either. Two hours later the current grew stronger and there were more unfamiliar bugs and insects being washed down the river. Usually worms appeared when the rains came. They had left their holes to explore the damp ground and suddenly found themselves caught up in water they couldn't navigate. That provided a new and interesting food for Lightning.

When the current brought the first worm near him, he grabbed a bit of it in his mouth and ate it. That tasted good! Another worm came along soon after. Lightning bit off a longer, fatter part of it. That was just as good. He swallowed and came back to get more but suddenly the worm was jerked out of the water. He looked around for it but couldn't see it anywhere. Then with a plop and lots of bubbles, a wriggling worm with a shiny spoon landed on the bottom near him.

The worm moved around but it didn't move along with the current. It just sat there and twisted uncomfortably around a sharp, pointy thing.

Lightning had grown used to catching his meals as they floated by in the stream. Anything that didn't move with the current made him suspicious. Suddenly the worm started to rise against the current in jerky motions. Interested by this surprising motion, Lightning approached. He was just about to grab the worm when it shot out of the water before he could get it in his mouth.

It was a good thing. That day was opening day of trout season.

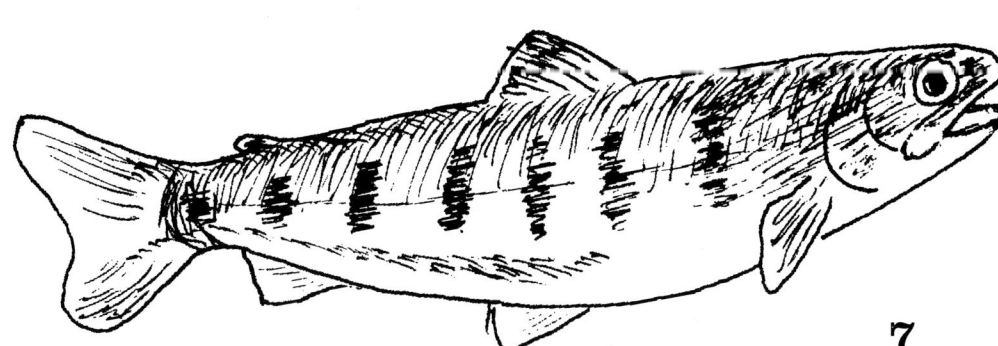

A few days later Lightning noticed another worm on the bottom of the pool. This worm wasn't floating in the current either, it just lay on the gravel and wiggled at him. He was hungry and the tail of the worm seemed to beckon to him teasingly. Then it disappeared.

A Close Call

Plop! It reappeared on the other side of the same rock on the bottom. Lightning, interested, swam over to inspect. He remembered how good worms were. The worm wriggled at him again. Too much to resist, he opened his mouth and swallowed.

When he bit down on it there was something unnaturally hard on his tongue. Before he could spit it out, he felt a sharp sting in his mouth and a jerk from above.

Lightning swam across the pool at full speed. The pull got stronger the farther away he swam. He dove down, then leaped out of the water, shaking his head to get rid of that hook. He hoped the crash of falling to the water would jar it free. No such luck. He shook his head one way, then the other. The hook held fast.

He dove down to the depths of the pool jerking his head from side to side. He wanted to stay down at the bottom where safety lay. The pull persisted. He could feel himself being drawn slowly towards the surface against his will. He swam in half circles now, as far away from the pull as he could. His muscles were starting to ache. He turned towards the pull for a moment and felt himself drawn towards the bank. Out of the corner of his eye Lightning saw a net reaching below him.

Panic gripped his heart. With a spurt of energy he swam as hard as he could for the bottom and his place of safety under the edge of a big boulder.

Without realizing it Lightning had swum under a branch of an old, submerged tree. The line got wedged tightly in a crack in the branch. Now he couldn't move at all! He thought his time had come. He shook his head hard. This time the line didn't budge but the hook loosened somewhat. With another jerk of his head the hook came out.

His mouth hurt. His heart was pounding but he was free! He slowly swam to the depths of the pool to recover. The straight, hard pull against the hook without the bend of the rod was all he needed to tear the hook out of his mouth.

On the other end of the line was Danny, a boy from the village who loved to fish. His line was now caught on the branch under water. No matter how much he bent his rod, the line held firm. He put the rod down and tugged on the line until, with a snap, it broke.

Disappointed, Danny reeled in his line. He slowly picked up his rod and can of worms and headed home. Instead of bringing home a glistening silvery trout with a rainbow on its side, he had a hollow, empty feeling in his heart. He swore to himself he'd catch that trout the next time!

Mayfly Hatch

When the spring grew warmer, the water insects became more plentiful. Lightning caught more nymphs as they left the gravelly bottom and floated to the surface. The hatchery trout had grown adept at finding nymphs, too. Drifting in the current underwater they were easy to catch, but at the surface they were even easier to eat.

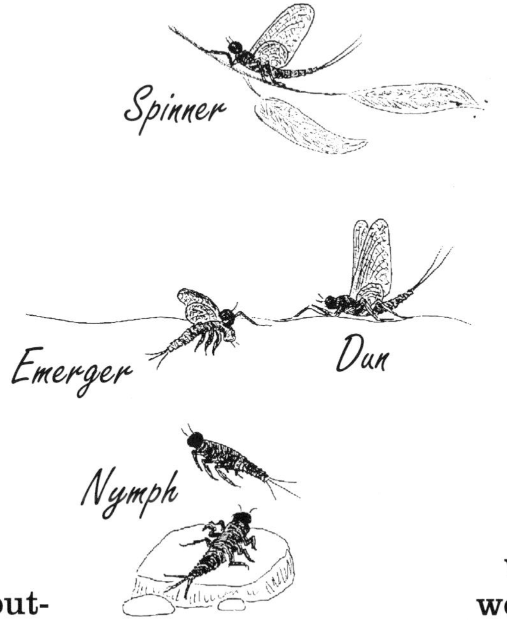

Once a nymph reached the surface, a strange transformation would take place. Out of the hard shell emerged a mayfly dun that would float for a minute on the current. There its wings would unfurl and dry before it could fly off into the air, leaving an empty nymph-like case behind on the water. Those seconds of wing drying were the easiest moment for the trout to grab it. Usually there weren't just one or two mayflies, either. They came suddenly in large numbers. They dotted the surface of the water before they flew off in the air.

Mayflies were delicious, crunchy on the outside, soft and gooey on the inside. Lightning gorged himself. The other trout ate their fill, too, but because of his size and speed he managed to get more than they did.

Afterwards he would return to the bottom of the pool, happily stuffed. Lightning was growing bigger and faster month by month.

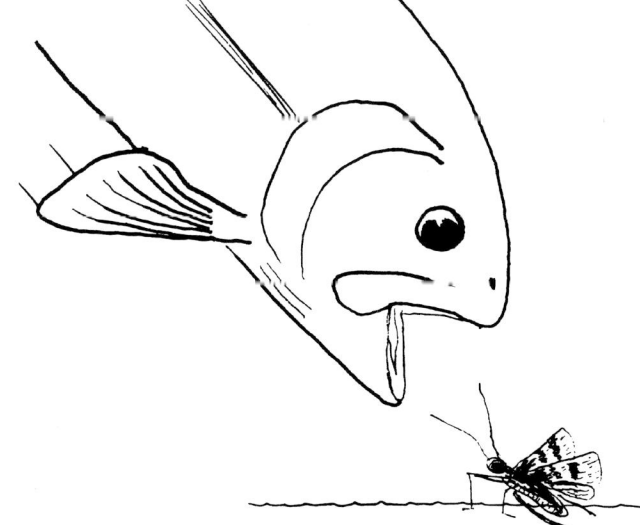

Spring was a bountiful time of year. Now when Lightning saw a worm he didn't even bother to investigate; there were too many good insects to eat.

In addition to the nymphs and mayflies, there were caddis flies that fluttered over the water. Sometimes, whole swarms pulsated up and down over the surface. As Lightning watched them, he would occasionally see one skitter and bounce across the surface film. With one leap he had that fly!

Danny returned to the stream often, his rod and worm can in his hand. He would get some of the new hatchery fish or sometimes nothing. Many of the stocked trout had already been taken for someone's dinner. They didn't have the caution and wariness of the native trout. In their innocence many more would be gone before their first winter in the stream.

Danny knew good fish were still there; he saw them rising to mayflies. Sometimes two or even three would jump at the same time. Yet, they just weren't as interested in his worms.

He often thought of the scrappy rainbow that he'd hooked earlier in the season that had fought so hard. If no one else had caught it by then, that fish was probably still in the same pool.

11

Summer's Heat

The dog days of summer came. Lightning usually felt like eating only in the cool of the evening or the dawn before another sultry day arrived. The rains were less frequent. The water became warmer and shallower and the sunlight stronger. There were fewer places to hide from being seen.

Lightning moved from the big pool he had grown to know so well, to another pool upstream where a smaller brook joined the main branch. Its waters felt cooler, for they flowed through a wooded valley where little sunlight ever warmed the rocks and water. The low water and the bright sun made Lightning yearn for the shadows and cool water of his home pool.

With the heat of summer came new insects to eat. Big yellow and green grasshoppers jumped from one clump of grass to another. Sometimes the wind caught them in flight or moved the grasses hanging over the stream. Any grasshopper missing its landing spot tumbled onto the water with a big splat! Kicking its legs to jump away, it made ripples in big rings on the surface. All that commotion woke Lightning out of his sleepy state. Just one grasshopper was quite a meal.

Occasionally an ant fell into the stream and struggled to reach land. Lightning swam effortlessly to the surface, ate it and returned to his place by the rock.

Flying ants came in swarms. When the wind dropped them on the stream, trout appeared from everywhere. The trout made the water boil until the ants were all gone.

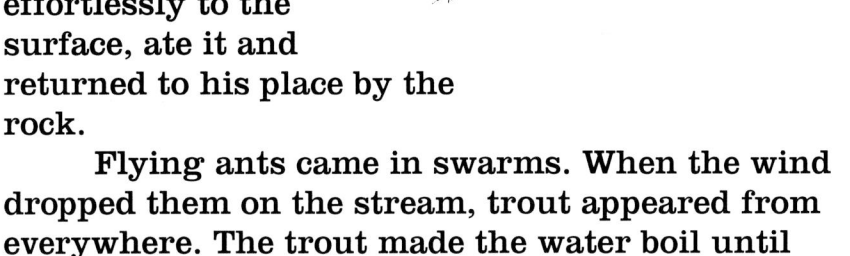

Summer was also the time when the dragonflies mated. On certain warm days of August, bright red-bodied dragonflies coupled in flight over the water. The two rose and fell together as they skimmed over the surface, the female's tail dipping into the water from time to time to deposit her eggs.

Their flight excited Lightning. He'd watch the direction they were flying and swim under water until, with a jump he'd come down on the dragonflies, his mouth wide-open.

He often caught them both and fell back into the water with a carefree splash. He was too happy to worry about being seen; that big mouthful of red dragonflies was worth it!

Summer Evening

On summer evenings tiny midges floated to the surface just as the mayfly nymphs had earlier in the year. He'd spot those tiny flies against the midnight blue of the night sky. Lightning would come to the surface, sip them as they changed from water insect to tiny fly and then gracefully submerge to wait for the next ones floating towards him.

On several occasions Grandpa, a fly fisherman who lived near the river, came in the evening to fish. He was retired and had time to do what he loved most—fly fishing. Rather than fish through the hottest part of the day when the trout were sluggish and uninspired, he came for the evening hatches. This was the best part of the day and he came well prepared. Boxes of flies bulged in the many pockets of his vest. He carried everything he might need from forceps to remove a hook, to bug repellant; from goop to make his flies float, to a flashlight to tie on the last fly of the evening.

Grandpa waded into the river and cast where the fish were rising. Sometimes the rises would stop as he waded in. Whether it was the sound his boots made when they crunched the gravel together or his tall, dark outline that warned the trout, he didn't know. Other times it was the shadow of his fishing line that spooked them, or the flies that didn't quite match the hatch.

Then there were the times when his fly was just right and the trout took it as quickly as they took the natural.

Whether he caught fish or not, he loved the challenge of casting: how to make the fly settle gently on the water just where he wanted, it was not easy. He had to keep the line taut should a trout stike, but be careful not to drag the fly across the current. He had to watch out not to hook the bushes on his back cast and to allow for the wind when it blew.

Was his fly what the trout were eating today? Could he make it land so gently on the water that a trout would believe it to be real? And when that didn't seem to be enough to interest a fish, could he tease a trout to strike 'cause the fly just might get away?

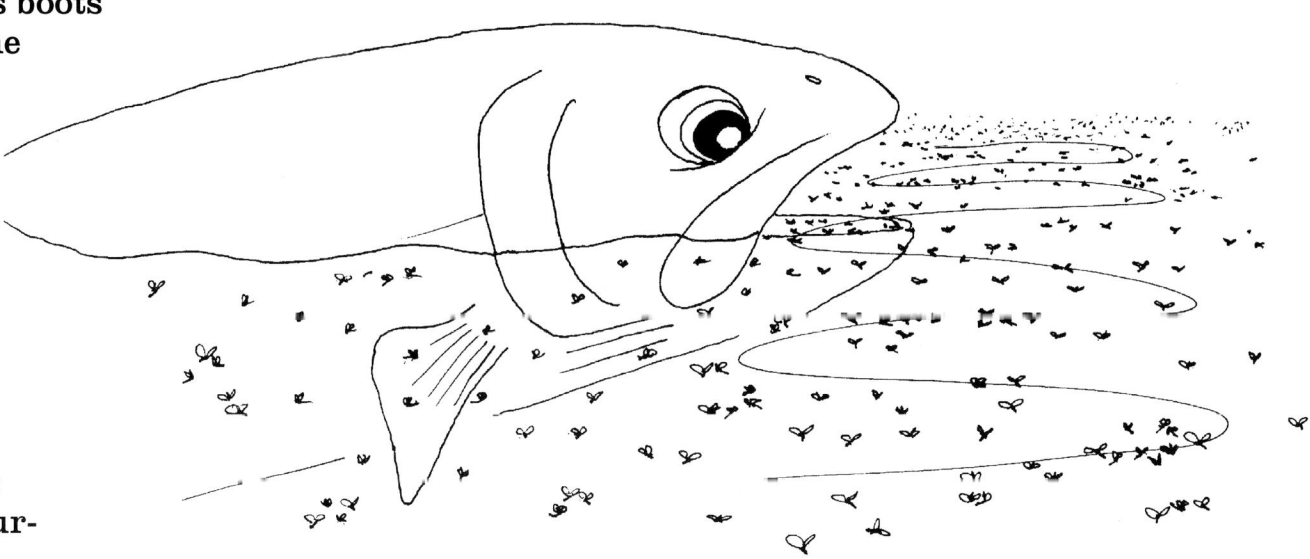

The End Of The Season

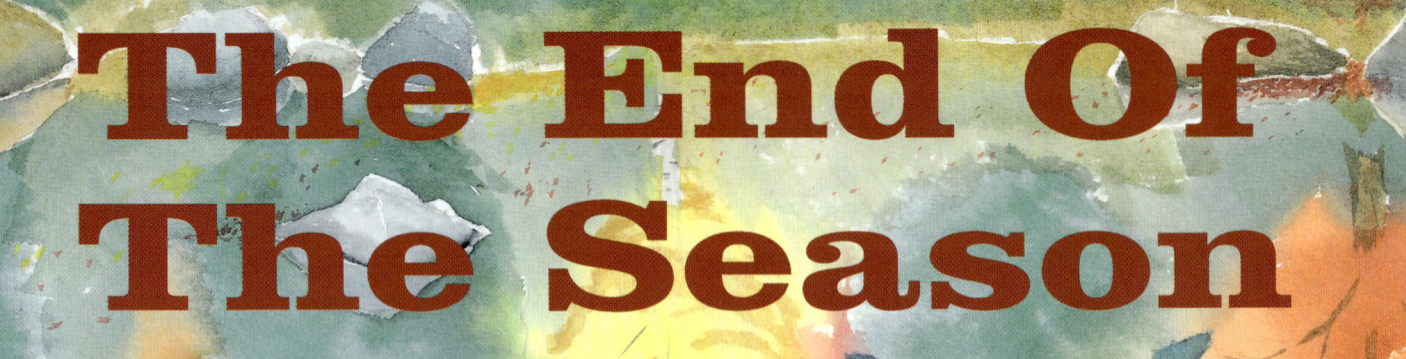

The mists rose off the river each morning as fall approached. The coolness of the water invigorated Lightning. He moved back to his home pool, now cooler and with a better supply of insects.

He had a strong urge to eat. Winter was approaching, and he needed all the fat he could put on. He had grown two inches longer during the summer. Now Lightning needed to get fatter.

Leaves of red, orange and gold fell on the pool's surface. The stream was carrying the fallen splendor of the autumn foliage. The eddies formed a dizzying spiral of crimson and yellow maple leaves.

Danny had gone back to school and become involved in sports. He thought little of the river now. Grandpa, on the other hand, spent more time than ever there. He loved the tapestry of rich colors that cloaked the hills and the warmth of the fall afternoons. He also knew the fishing season would soon be over. Each day became more special.

As the days passed, Grandpa's flies caught more trout than they had all summer. Even Lightning was about to gobble one down until at the last second it didn't seem right to him. Real flies float exactly where the current takes them. This imitation of Grandpa's seemed to be going across the flow and left ripple marks behind it. It wasn't like the other flies. Lightning's natural caution held him back from sampling it.

On the last day of trout fishing Grandpa hoped to catch that big rainbow as a fitting end to the season. He had watched Lightning rise many times in the big pool. He had often looked for Lightning's shadow on the floor of the pool and then been able to spot the big trout.

Grandpa had barely begun his cast, when a beaver saw him and slapped the water with a heavy, flat tail. Splash! The beaver warned his cubs of a man on the river. That warning told all the river's inhabitants, animals and fish, to beware. Lightning did not overlook the warning.

That afternoon Grandpa headed home without a fish. He was content to have spent so many happy hours on the river he loved. He was sad that the season was over but the bite of the cold weather made him look forward to the warmth of his cozy home through the long, cold winter months ahead.

A Hungry Otter

Even though Grandpa no longer was fishing, all of Lightning's dangers had not gone away for the winter. An otter, who was also trying to fatten up before the winter, caught sight of him. Lightning was swimming just enough to stay still, about a foot below the surface.

The otter ran around the rocks until he was standing just above Lightning. In a flash he dove on top of him, his mouth half open to catch him.

When Lightning saw the otter he did what he always did in case of danger: he swam down towards the bottom and his place of safety.

Frustrated at missing his prey, the otter pursued the trout to the bottom. Lightning then raced to the other end of the pool, the otter swimming just behind him. When the trout made a sharp turn, the otter swung wide. Lightning made a couple more sharp turns around the boulders he knew so well. The otter had to go up for breath.

Lightning hid in the dark shadows but it was only a minute before the otter's head appeared from around a rock bearing down on him. Startled and scared, Lightning raced the length of the pool and through the rapids into a smaller, narrow pool above.

The otter climbed out around the rapids, caught his breath and then dove into the smaller pool. Here the otter had the advantage. There were fewer boulders and it was much shallower.

The otter was closing in. He was ready for Lightning. With a sudden spurt of energy Lightning made a sharp turn to the left, and swam as fast as he could with the otter right behind. Lightning crossed the pool and came to the rapids. He didn't question which way would be safer; he plunged down them and back into his home pool.

Winded, the otter stopped at the rapids. Lightning had disappeared in the deeper pool again. How could he corner that slippery fish this time? He couldn't think of a good answer, the otter shook his coat and looked for other trout.

Most of the hatchery trout had been caught by the heron, a fish hawk or some of the many fishermen who came to catch their suppers. Not seeing anything he could catch easily, the otter trotted off.

Meanwhile Lightning waited for the next attack, his heart pounding. This time he hid under a log where his natural colors helped him become almost invisible. The patches of sunlight and shadow further blended his colors with those of the log, the rocks and the water. By evening he felt reassured and hungry enough to return to his feeding spot to see what would come floating down the current to eat.

Lightning did not easily forget that deadly game of tag.

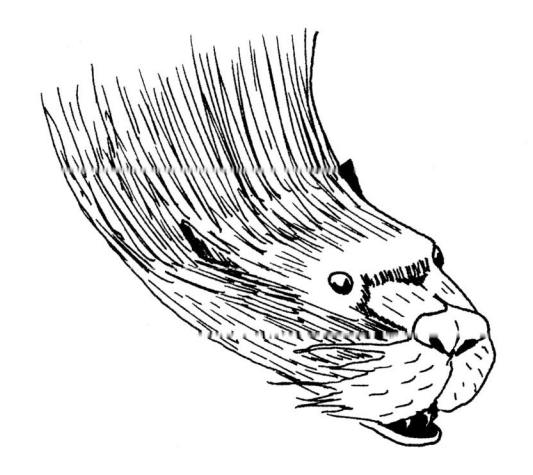

The Winter Freeze

Winter came suddenly that year. The skin of ice that coated the still waters had formed nightly from mid-October on. By December the ice was firmly established on the river's edge; only the speed of the current kept it from covering the whole river.

With the sinking temperatures came a slowing down of Lightning's body. His temperature was the same as the water's, he swam much less, ate less because he needed less. He even breathed less because the colder water held more oxygen.

He spent much of his day now right next to the river bottom behind a boulder where he needed the least amount of exertion to swim. When he became hungry, he would look for the water insects whose movements were also slowed down. Occasionally a minnow or a small trout would get too close and provide him dinner.

As the ice overhead thickened and the snow fell, the open area where the current was flowing grew smaller. There was less and less light in Lightning's world. What there was came in long shafts on the rare sunny days.

In his own way Lightning was hibernating. He wasn't asleep, curled up in a ball like a bear, raccoon or a woodchuck, but everything had slowed down in his body. He had found a spot where the back current held him gently up against a large boulder where he hardly had to swim at all.

The ice grew thicker not only above him but also below him. Anchor ice formed on the bottom because the ground had grown colder than the flowing water. The blue-green ice was growing from the bottom up. It started to wall him off from the current in his spot behind the boulder. In his numb, almost frozen, sleepy state it was difficult for him to recognize the danger of the encircling ice. Each day as the ice grew thicker above and below him, he moved to prevent freezing in. As his body temperature was the same as the water that surrounded him he grew cold and numb. He was waiting for the days to pass. The winter months seemed to drag on without end.

Imitation Mayflies

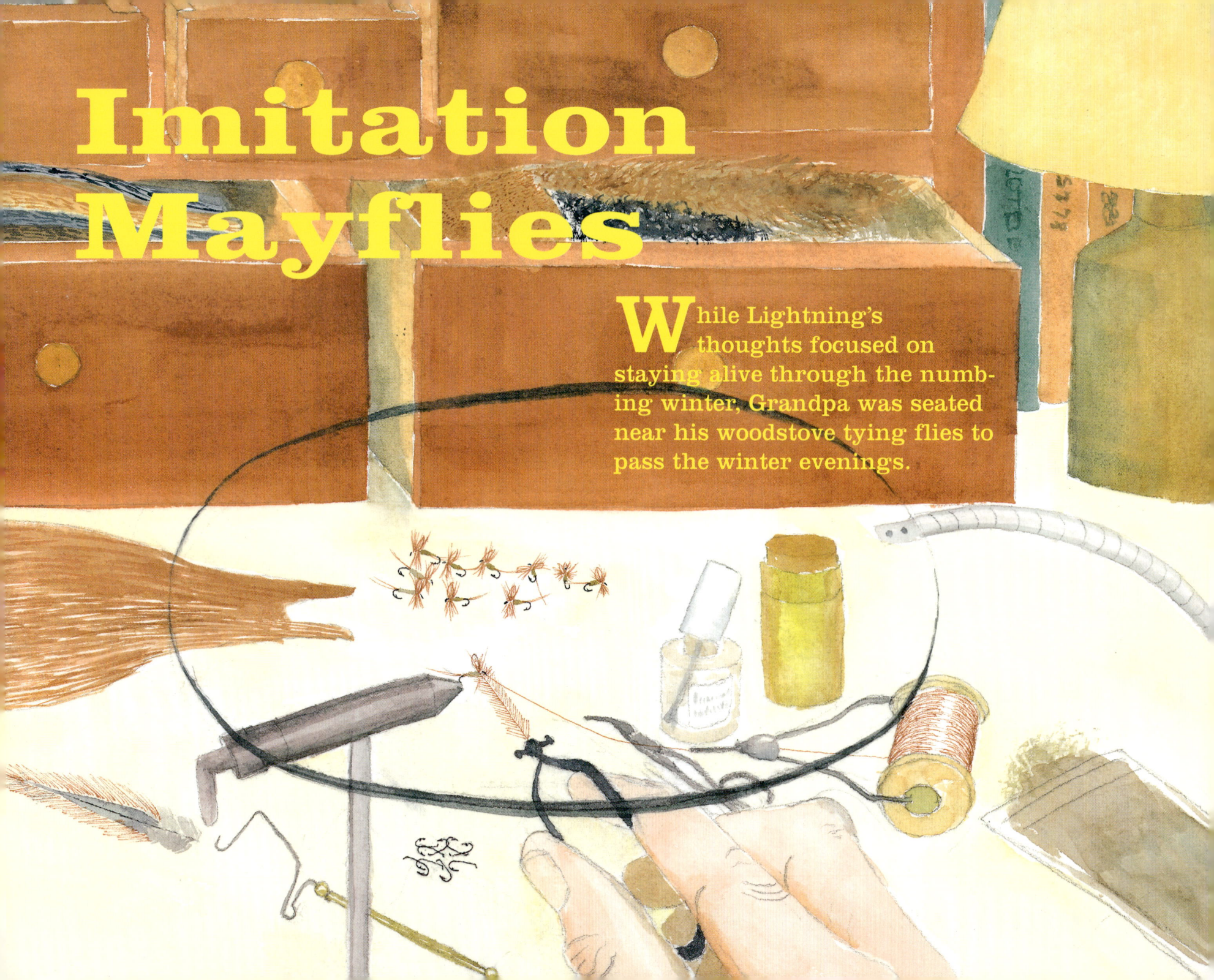

While Lightning's thoughts focused on staying alive through the numbing winter, Grandpa was seated near his woodstove tying flies to pass the winter evenings.

He used feathers, fur, thread and glue to turn a bare hook into a mayfly that was so real it all but flew away.

He'd start off with a tiny bunch of feathers to make the antennae. Then he'd spin rabbit fur onto a sticky thread and wind it on the hook to make the insect's body. As he went along he glued the thread as he finished each part of the fly. He tied two tiny hackles from the neck of a rooster upright to form the mayfly's wings.

A long, narrow rooster feather went on next. He wound it around the hook just before the eye. That feather created the impression of wings in motion. He tied several knots to hold it in a neat winding at the eye of the hook.

After he'd glued it, he admired it with satisfaction. The shape, the outline, the way the fly sat up looked as if it had been a nymph just minutes before. "Aha! This one's good enough to fool that big rainbow!" As Grandpa tied an especially lifelike fly he thought of that fish. Everything would need to be just right to catch that one.

After an evening of tying, more than a dozen flies sat so lightly on his table top, it looked as though a hatch had just emerged, their wings drying and whirring, ready for flight.

Grandpa was happy tying flies. There were always new materials and new ideas to try. And questions without answers such as: What did an insect look like to a trout? How much detail really made a difference in a fly? Why do some flies work well when they don't even look like any particular insect?

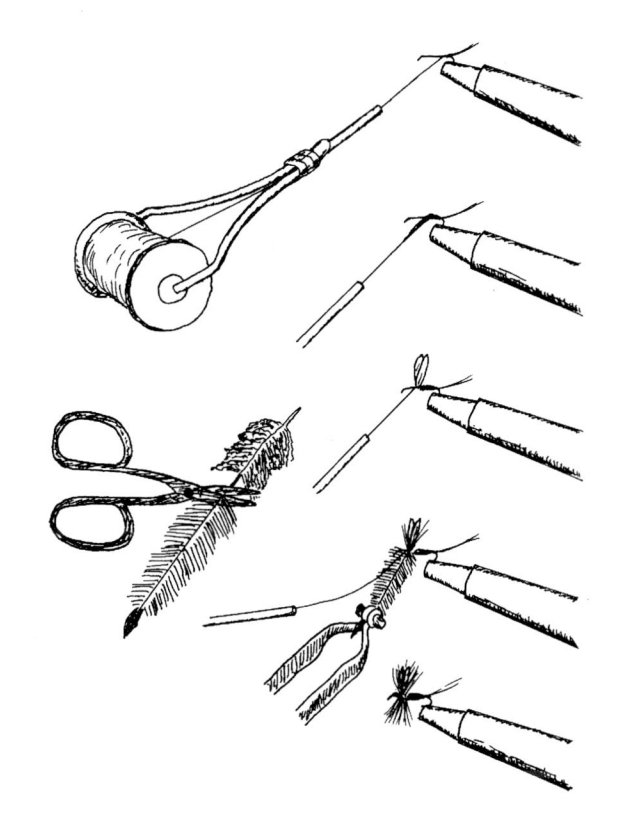

Not only were there mayflies of different colors and sizes to tie, but midges, caddisflies and nymphs as well. Then there were the grasshoppers, crickets and ants. There seemed to be no end of patterns and sizes he needed for his many fly boxes for next season.

Grasshopper   *Cricket*   *Ant*

Spring Break Up

Just when it seemed that the anchor ice from the bottom was going to meet the ice from the surface of the stream and squeeze out the last flowing water, the weather changed. It wasn't a gradual change but a sudden warming in February that melted the snow, flooded the brooks and turned the water coffee-colored.

Muddy flood waters pushed the ice from underneath. Suddenly it cracked, shattered and broke into cakes that were carried downstream in the wild tumult of an early spring break up. More chunks of ice were ripped off, as the water tore open the ice that covered the river.

Lightning had to swim hard now to find a sheltered spot. With anchor ice changing the shape of the bottom, and the sudden surge of water, his once peaceful world had become topsy-turvy and threatened to carry him off downstream in the flood.

Careening, cavorting ice cakes crunched into one another with grinding shocks. Occasionally a cake would slice the water above him, and slam into the rocks so hard the water tremors bounced from bank to bank.

As the flood waters passed downstream, ice blocks piled up on the banks. They tumbled, higgledy-piggledy one on top of another. Some of the cakes were jagged arrowheads, others square, some rounded by cracking into the rocks.

Whatever their shape, they were all formed by the same winter. They all had the same layered sequence of the winter's cold spells and storms. They were like many-sided cookies cut from the same sheet of dough. They were all children of the same winter.

The extra swimming was tiring for Lightning, who had eaten little all winter long. The fat he had been able to add in autumn had served as an energy source when there was little else. The water bugs were often frozen under the anchor ice. There weren't any land bugs now. He did find a young trout or a minnow now and then, but his body was living on whatever he had stored up in the fall.

Food Finally

As the sun's rays grew stronger, March became April and the snow melted. The water running down the valley began to warm up. The sun's rays grew stronger and finally, there were bugs to eat. Lightning's appetite had never been keener after the winter's fast. When something to eat appeared he grabbed it without question. It was food.

Occasionally chunks of anchor ice would break loose from the bottom, float to the surface and bob down the river. Imbedded in their underside were rocks, nymphs and gravel.

As the cakes of ice floated downstream, they scoured the banks and the shallow waters, destroying more of Lightning's food. The high water, the destruction and the scouring of the river bed made it much harder for Lightning to find anything to eat.

Migrating ducks appeared on the river now looking for food as they travelled north. Green-headed, white and black mergansers stopped over on the river to feed and regain strength before flying on. Skilled divers and catchers of small fish, they chased the minnows and small trout.

With spring, however, came the warmth that caused the rebirth of insect life. Nature supplied Lightning with food when he needed it most. Nymphs started to move about in the gravel. They moved stiffly, no match for hungry Lightning. They seemed tastier than ever. As the ground was no longer frozen, even worms started to float downstream.

Lightning's hunger did not go away easily; it had built up during the long, lean winter.

Lightning Gets Big

And so the years passed. Lightning grew in length and weight. He had learned to be suspicious of everything that looked unnatural. Fussier about what he ate, he was also suspicious of anything that could hurt him.

The sound of a man's footsteps on the bank spooks him now for half an hour. When looking up from the bottom he can spot a careless fisherman who walks near the bank of the stream, unaware how visible he is.

When Lightning eats, it is usually underwater on the nymphs, minnows, worms and occasional crayfish that he catches as they come by, carried in the current. He prefers to eat in the evening when dangers are fewer. However, a good hatch of mayflies or midges draws him to the surface. Then he gently breaks the surface film, swallows the fly and returns to his post.

The sudden shadow of a fisherman's line on the surface of the water overhead tips him off to danger. Most importantly, he knows that flies only drift freely in the current. If a fisherman's leader drags the fly sidewise ever so slightly, it is not to be sampled.

He occasionally takes an unfamiliar bug or fly into his mouth and examines it gently. If it doesn't seem good or natural he spits it out. Most of the time Lightning is so skillful and quick that a fisherman doesn't even know that his fly has been inside a trout's mouth.

Because Lightning is so aware of the dangers that threaten his life, he is the largest trout in that part of the river. He is strong enough to drive away any challengers from the best feeding spots. That enables him to eat more and with greater safety. He is becoming an exceptional trout.

Spawning

With spring comes the time to spawn. He feels a compelling urge to be with a female trout. There are one or two females his size but one who seems to accept him more than the others.

When she swims to the gravelly brook he enjoyed last summer, Lightning follows her. There she turns on her side and flaps her tail back and forth rapidly until she makes a hollow or "redd" in the gravel. The larger gravel is pushed aside by her tail. The resulting hollow is lined with small pebbles. During this time Lightning waits just downstream of the redd.

Once the nest is completed, he swims beside her, rubbing her with his snout. At one particular moment they both arch their backs. She deposits hundreds of eggs into the gravel bed and he sprays them with milt. She swims upstream again and flaps her tail until the eggs are covered with fine gravel.

They do this several times in the next day or two until both are exhausted.

Thinner and tired they return downstream, badly in need of food and rest. Nature's bounty of insects restores them.

With May there are more hatches and the feasting lasts all day long. Lightning eats the mayflies as they emerge from their nymph bodies. The hatched mayfly duns sit on the surface for an instant before they fly off into their new world of air, color and sunlight.

The Encounter

Lightning is so busy gorging himself on mayflies that he doesn't even look at Danny's worm wriggling on the bottom. Nor does he hear a fisherman who walks quietly to the edge of the river.

For Grandpa this is the kind of hatch he'd waited for. He catches a mayfly in his hand as it floats towards him on the surface of the stream, studies it and then looks into his fly box to find a similarly colored fly of matching size. One of those he'd tied last winter is just right. The shade of the body and wings is perfect; it is just a bit longer than the natural but close enough. He needs to cast it upstream from the trout and float it over the spot where the trout is feeding.

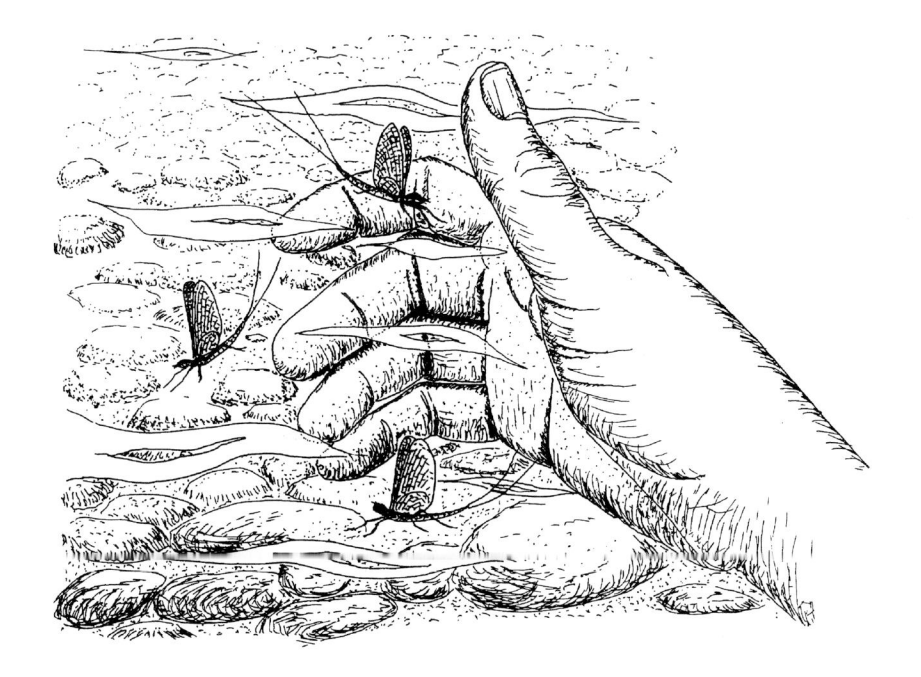

He wades carefully into the lower end of the pool. With each step he feels his way along the slippery rocks, as he watches the fish continue to rise. He holds his breath, hoping the fish won't become aware of him. Grandpa casts a few times in the air to get out enough line and then lets his fly settle on the water, delicately.

As it floats over the trout's feeding spot, a fish's head breaks the surface and a split second later the fly disappears.

The sting of the hook in Lightning's mouth electrifies him. He bolts upstream. The rod doubles over. Line screams off Grandpa's reel.

The Fight

Lightning turns, jumps clear of the water and falls heavily on his side.

"Hey!" Grandpa cried to himself, full of admiration for Lightning's strength and size. "That's the big rainbow!"

The jump has not dislodged the hook. The fish heads for the big boulder at the bottom of the pool. This time however, the old branch that had saved Lightning before had been scoured away by the ice when it went out of the river in the spring.

From below, Lightning shoots two feet out of the water. In the air he shakes his body to rid himself of that pull in his mouth. He falls, kersplash, still hooked.

Danny, who heard the scream of Grandpa's reel, comes to see what was happening. "Wow! That's the big rainbow!" he says half out loud. Danny's eyes bug out as he sees Lightning race the length of the pool. What a fish!

Down Lightning dives to the base of the rock wall. Below the surface a good five feet, the trout shakes his head against the pull of the rod. The line cuts through the water, throbbing with Lightning's every move.

Another surge to the head of the pool. This time the trout has less energy than before. The current and the bend of the rod are weighing on him, slowing him down. He turns, unable to fight both.

Lightning makes several short spurts towards the middle of the pool. The rod dips and arches but he doesn't manage to take much line from the reel. When Lightning slows down, the rod rises slowly in the air as it pulls him closer to the surface. But Lightning far prefers the safety of the depths of the pool. He uses his weight to his advantage and swims across the pool, boring deeper in the current as he swims. Whenever Lightning slows his efforts, the rod brings him closer to the surface slowly.

Grandpa takes the landing net hanging from his back and cautiously slips it in the water in front of him. When Lightning sees the net out of the corner of his eye he makes a last desparate run. The line pulsates as it cuts through the water. But now Lightning's weight isn't enough to keep him down and he doesn't have any reserve strength left to try to swim lower.

All he can do is swim in semi-circles, first one way then the other. He doesn't want to get any closer to that man than he has to.

"Danny," says Grandpa, "You take my net. I'll head him towards you."

Danny grabs the net and stands on a rock ledge that sticks out into the water. Lightning goes first one way then the other. Each time he comes near Danny, the boy tries to get the net under Lightning's heavy body, but each time with a quick flick of his tail Lightning swims out of reach.

The bowed rod and the length of the battle are telling, however. Finally Grandpa keeps Lightning's head out of water so he can't see the net. Danny is reaching towards him. As Grandpa leads Lightning toward the boy, Danny scoops the big fish up in the net.

A rush of relief and joy floods over Grandpa—he has finally caught that beautiful rainbow!

Grandpa puts down his rod, takes the net, wets his hand and reaches in for Lightning. The trout flip-flops back and forth in Grandpa's grasp until Grandpa manages to hold him firmly upside down.

Questions

"I'll get that hook out just as gently as I can," says Grandpa as he looks in Lightning's mouth. "Just hold still."

With his forceps, Grandpa grasps the tiny hook and removes it from the corner of Lightning's mouth. Danny watches the operation without a word.

Once the fly is out Grandpa turns Lightning right side up to admire him. "Look at those colors, Danny. Isn't he a beauty?"

"I never saw one as big as that. He's huge!" says Danny.

"And he didn't give up easily, either. Did you see him jump?"

"Yeah. I saw him. He's a fighter!" Danny says with admiration.

"He had to be to live through the cold winters, the spring floods and to avoid the many mouths that wanted him for dinner, you know. A trout that big is really special."

Danny soaks up that fish with his eyes so as not to forget him. Grandpa too. He even thinks he might have him mounted. That trout would look handsome over his fly tying desk.

"But you know," says Grandpa thoughtfully, "if I put him back in the river he'll be there another day for you...or me. Wouldn't you like to have a chance to catch him too?"

Danny's heart jumps. "You bet I would," he says with a smile that goes around his face.

Grandpa puts the big fish back in the water and holds him with two hands. He moves Lightning back and forth to get his gills opening and closing and his breathing more regular.

Grandpa admires the dark green color of Lightning's back, the fins that seem so filmy yet are so strong and the red of his gills as they open and close.

After a minute, when the trout is breathing regularly, Grandpa slowly opens his hands. With two or three flicks of the tail, the trout glides over the gravel and disappears in the deep green waters of the stream.

Adams   *Royal Wulff*

Grandpa and Danny walk up from the river that day empty-handed but excited. The memory of the fight still fresh in their minds, they share special parts of the last 15 minutes that they never will forget.

Danny is already hoping for a chance to catch that rainbow. He wants to learn how to fool a good fish with a fly.

He turns to Grandpa and asks, "Will you teach me how to tie a fly, Grandpa?"

Given the circumstances the author very much believes in catch and release!